# Kid in the Q
## ...what a pandemic

KRISTIAN DANIELS

To order additional copies of this book, contact:
Xlibris
844-714-8691
www.Xlibris.com
Orders@Xlibris.com

ISBN:    Softcover        978-1-6641-8044-4
         EBook            978-1-6641-8043-7

Print information available on the last page

Rev. date: 06/16/2021

# Kid in the Q

## ...what a pandemic

One day in March 2020, I stop having to wake up at 7:00 a.m. every day. Neither one of my parents has breakfast ready, and my clothes aren't laid out for school. A day home with my brother, mom, and dad? Awesome! Sure, I like my teacher, but what child would not rather still be in bed past seven o'clock?

After a couple of weeks of staying home, I yell downstairs, "Mom, when do I go back to school?"

"Kamili, I told you that the state is on a stay-at-home order. No school for you or other kids. Everyone will be quarantining."

"I'm five years old. I don't really understand what quarantine is."

Mom replies, "You will continue to be home with your family, away from the public, including church. We don't know how long you will be home with us."

"Okay, Mom. How about we make a list of fun things we can do as a family?"

"Kamili, that's a prodigious idea. Let's ask your brother what he thinks. Later, we can FaceTime cousin Olivia to see what she is doing while she quarantines."

Our quarantine list:

- Morning wash
- Breakfast
- Learning
- Break
- Outdoor planting

Okay, mom I think I have covered everything for our quarantine list.

I have still not returned to school or the playground. Every time we go into the store, Mother tells me to put on my mask. It seems cool, but after a couple of minutes, my ears start to hurt. I don't know how much more I can take of this!

# Grocery Store

My mom says my mauntie is coming to visit us in a week, and I cannot wait. She always has fun activities for my brother and me to do.

There's was a knock at the door. It's both my aunts. Before they can come in the house, my dad sprays them and their belongings with a can of "go away, germs."

My quarantine days are getting better now that there are more relatives in the house. We have morning jogs and make Jell-O; Daddy manages the grill, and Mommy works in the kitchen.

The phone rings. "What great news!" I hear my mom say.

"Mother, Mother, what's the great news?"

"Kamili, childcare centers are opening back up."

"Yay! Should I go to bed now?"

"No, silly; you still have two more weeks home with your family."

On Monday, July 20, I am finally back in the classroom with my teacher and a few of my friends. COVID-19 is still present, so we are instructed to social distance, that is, to stay six feet apart from one another. It's not easy, but it's better than another quarantine day at home.

### *Spicy New Phrases and Words*

- stay-at-home order–to remain at home
- quarantine– time period of being away from common public places.
- social distance–personal space of 6 ft.
- prodigious–remarkable
- mauntie–an aunt that is like a mom

CPSIA information can be obtained
at www.ICGtesting.com
Printed in the USA
BVHW020042011021
617793BV00002B/54